SUMMER MAGIC

by RUTH CHEW

Illustrated by the author

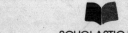
SCHOLASTIC INC.
New York Toronto London Auckland Sydney Tokyo

ISBN 0-590-10421-7

15 14 13 12 11 10 9 8 7 6 5   4 5 6 7 8/8

Printed in the U.S.A.   01

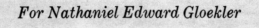

For Nathaniel Edward Gloekler

"Play fair, Sarah! You said you'd let me look at the mummy." Timothy Standish yanked at his sister's hand.

Sarah made a face. She wasn't as fond of mummies as her brother was.

It was Sunday afternoon. Sarah and Timothy were walking through Prospect Park. They were on their way to the Brooklyn Museum.

When they came to the zoo in the park, Sarah wanted to look at the animals.

"It's too hot to go inside the animal houses," Timothy said.

"Most of the animals are in the outside cages today," Sarah told him.

Sarah and Timothy watched the sea

lions splashing in their pool. "I wish *we* could go swimming," Timothy said.

"Maybe it's cooler in the Botanic Garden." Sarah led the way across Flatbush Avenue to the garden on the other side.

They walked past the fountain and the water-lily pond. Sarah stopped to smell a funny crinkly flower. It grew on a bush near the gate that led to the parking lot of the Brooklyn Museum. She caught sight of a metal sign.

"Musk rose, an ancient rose," Sarah read. "Tim, smell this."

Timothy stuck his nose into the flower. Then he grabbed the rose and pulled it off the bush.

"Hey there, boy, stop that!" One of the men who worked in the Garden came running over. "I'll have to ask you to leave."

The man watched to make sure that

Timothy and Sarah went out by the gate. Then he went back to weeding the herb garden.

Sarah was angry. "Tim, how could you do that? You know you're not allowed to pick the flowers in there."

"I'm sorry, Sarah. I don't know why I did it. Somehow I couldn't seem to stop myself." Timothy handed his sister the little pink flower. "Here, you take the rose. I don't want it now."

It made Sarah feel guilty to hold the flower, just as if she had been the one to pick it. But she didn't want the little rose to die. She stuck it in the top buttonhole of her shirt. "I'll put it in water when we get home."

The children crossed the parking lot to the back door of the museum. Then they went inside.

"At least it's cool in here," Tim said.

They had to go through the gift shop

to get to the elevator. Sarah wanted to stop and see the dolls from different countries.

"Promise we'll go and find the mummy next," Tim said.

"I promise." Sarah bent over a case to look at a wooden doll from Sweden.

Before Timothy could get her to leave the gift shop, she looked at all the dolls in the case.

They took the elevator upstairs. The elevator man let them off on the fourth floor. Timothy looked around. "There's no mummy here. These are just cases full of old furniture and clothes. Let's get back on the elevator."

Sarah went over to look at an old-fashioned dress in one of the cases.

"Come on," Tim said.

The children turned to go back to the elevator. Suddenly Timothy grabbed Sarah's arm. "Hey, look at that!"

Sarah turned and saw what seemed to be a whole house inside the museum.

Timothy went over and peeked through the small square panes of glass in one of the windows. "There's a big fireplace in there."

Sarah came to join her brother. She put her nose against the ripply glass. "Look at the big pot hanging on that hook. Wouldn't it be fun if we could go into the house?"

Timothy stepped back from the window. He caught sight of a small glass case on one wall of the museum. "Sarah, here's a picture of this house with trees around it."

Sarah went to look at it. The house was the same, all right. It was long and low, with gray clapboard walls and a shingled roof. A sign under the drawing read *House on Mill Island, Flatlands, Brooklyn, 1675.*

"1675. That means this house is more than three hundred years old," Sarah told Timothy.

He left the case and walked around the corner of the house. "Sarah," he called. "Here's a door. And it's open!"

Sarah raced around to where Timothy was. Together they crowded through the door into the house.

Smack! About two feet inside the house they were stopped by a glass wall. They could see into the room. But they couldn't go into it.

Sarah looked through the glass wall at the wide boards on the floor, at the long table with heavy legs, and at the tall grandfather clock. In the corner a bed was built into the wall. It was like a cupboard without doors. There were curtains to pull in front of it. Sarah wondered what it would be like to sleep in a bed like that.

Timothy wrinkled his nose. "What's that funny smell, Sarah?"

Sarah sniffed the air. She remembered the smell from somewhere. Then she looked down and caught sight of the crinkly little rose in her buttonhole. "Maybe it's this." She pulled the flower out of her shirt and held it to Timothy's nose.

"That's it, all right." Timothy sniffed the rose for a minute. "I wonder if the smell gets stronger if you crush it." He rubbed the flower against the glass wall in front of them.

The smell got stronger and stronger. It almost made Sarah's head ache. "Stop it, Tim!" She reached out to grab the rose away from him.

Timothy ducked. He stepped forward. The glass had turned to air. And he could walk right through it. Before she knew what she was doing Sarah had chased her brother into the room. He dodged away from her. Sarah stubbed her toe on one of the heavy legs of the long table.

"Ow!" Sarah stopped and looked around. Everything seemed different.

The pendulum on the tall clock was swinging back and forth. And the clock was ticking loudly. Somewhere outside the window a rooster crowed.

Timothy looked for the flower he had been holding. It was nowhere to be seen. "Sarah, what's happened? Let's get out of here." Timothy grabbed her hand and pulled her back to the open door.

Sarah half expected to be trapped in the room by the glass wall. But the wall was gone. The two children stepped out of the door onto a long, low stoop in front of the house.

Sarah couldn't believe her eyes. "Tim," she whispered, "we're outdoors!"

"It smells like the seaside," Timothy said.

"It *is* the seaside, Tim. Look!" Sarah pointed across a dirt road that ran in front of the house.

There was a marshy field with sand dunes on the other side of it. Beyond the sand dunes the sea sparkled in the afternoon sunlight.

A creek flowed through the salt marshes and between the dunes. There was a dam over the creek to make a pond. And a mill had been built right on the beach. Timothy and Sarah could hear a steady splashing sound as the big mill wheel turned.

Then they heard something else.

Far down the road there was a rattling, clanking noise. Around the bend came a wagon pulled by a chunky horse. There were two people riding in the wagon.

Sarah and Timothy stepped off the stoop into the road. They watched the wagon come nearer and nearer.

A man was driving. He wore a wide-brimmed black hat. The woman beside him had a white cap on her head.

The man waved. "Greetings," he called to the children.

Timothy and Sarah waved back. But they didn't say anything.

When the wagon reached the house, the man pulled hard on the reins. "Whoah!"

The horse stopped. The man and the woman climbed down from the wagon. Now the children saw that the man was wearing baggy knee breeches and the woman had skirts down to her ankles.

Sarah tried not to stare. She thought the man and the woman were also trying not to look too hard at the clothes she and Timothy wore.

The woman came forward and held out her hand. She was not young, but her cheeks were still pink and round. And her eyes were bright blue. "I'm Vrouw Maarten," she said.

Sarah shook hands. "My name is Sarah Standish. This is my brother Timothy."

Vrouw Maarten shook hands with Tim. "You must be English," she said. "Do you live in Gravesend?"

The only Gravesend Timothy knew was Gravesend Bay. He was sure she didn't mean that. "No," he said.

The man was opening the big front door of the barn that stood beside the house. Timothy ran to help. The man unhitched the gray horse. Then he tied him to a fence post where the horse could munch the rough grass that grew beside the road. Timothy helped push the high-backed wagon into the barn.

Vrouw Maarten walked over. "Hendrick," she said, "I see you've made friends with Timothy."

Sarah was following close behind the plump housewife. Vrouw Maarten turned to her. "This is my husband, Heer Maarten. Hendrick, this is Sarah."

Heer Maarten had a kind face. It was

brown and wrinkled. And the blue of his eyes was faded from the sun. When he took off his hat Sarah saw that his blond hair was turning gray.

She was going to hold out her hand. But Heer Maarten bowed to her. So instead of shaking hands Sarah made the little curtsey she had learned for the dance festival in school. It was hard to curtsey when she was wearing jeans.

Timothy was looking into the barn. He pointed to a row of small holes up near the eaves. "What are those for?"

"For the birds to come in and out by," Vrouw Maarten told him. "See, they have nests up there under the roof."

Sarah stepped into the barn and craned her neck to see better.

"It's nice to have company," Heer Maarten said. "Come inside. Jannetje and I have just come from church." He led the way into the house.

While Heer Maarten and his wife went into the back room to change out of their best clothes, Sarah and Timothy sat down at the long table. Timothy looked at the floor. "There's sand on it," he said. "I didn't notice that when we were in the museum. Everything's different."

"Yes," Sarah said. "Don't you see what's happened?"

Timothy shook his head.

"We've gone back into the past," Sarah said. "It may be three hundred years before our time. This is the way the house looked in the picture."

Timothy thought about this. Then he asked, "How are we going to get back where we belong?"

"I wish I knew," his sister told him.

Vrouw Maarten came back into the room. She was wearing a white apron over a blue dress. "Sarah," she said, "I don't mean to be rude. But I can't help wondering how you children came here. You are very welcome. Still I know your mother must be worried about you."

Sarah looked into Vrouw Maarten's blue eyes. "I'm not sure how we got here," she said. "And I don't know how to let my mother know where we are. If you want me to tell you what happened, I will. But you won't believe me."

Vrouw Maarten looked hard at Sarah. Then she turned to Timothy. "What do you have to say?"

Timothy had a feeling they were in trouble. "It's my fault," he said. "I pushed my way into your house."

Vrouw Maarten frowned. "Just a minute," she said. She went to the door that led to the back room. "Hendrick, come here."

Heer Maarten came into the big kitchen-living room. He had changed into soft leather shoes, and he was smoking a long-stemmed pipe. "What's the matter, Jannetje?"

Vrouw Maarten sat down at the long table. "The children have a strange story to tell. I'd like you to hear it too."

Heer Maarten smiled at Sarah and Timothy. "Don't be afraid," he said. "I was young once myself." He sat down beside his wife. "Now let's hear all about it."

Sarah swallowed. She knew Heer Maarten would think she was lying. Tears came into her eyes. Vrouw Maarten reached across the table and patted her hand.

"It seems a long time ago," Sarah started. "But I guess it hasn't happened yet. We had just finished lunch when Mother thought it might be a good idea if we went to the park for the afternoon."

"What park, dear?" Vrouw Maarten asked.

"Prospect Park, the big park in the middle of Brooklyn," Timothy said.

"Oh, you come from Breuckelen!" Vrouw Maarten said. "I didn't know there was a park in Breuckelen."

"Hush, Jannetje," Heer Maarten said. "Let the children tell their story. We'll ask questions afterward."

Together Timothy and Sarah told

what had happened to them that afternoon. Much of the time Sarah was sure that the Maartens didn't know what they were talking about. But Heer Maarten and his wife sat across from them at the table and listened until the story was done. Then Vrouw Maarten got up and walked around the table. She put her hand on Sarah's forehead just as her mother did when she thought Sarah had a fever.

"They seem to believe their story, Hendrick," she said to her husband.

Heer Maarten looked at the sneakers and blue jeans Sarah and Timothy were wearing. "When I was a boy in the old country," he said, "we used to gather around the fireside on a winter evening and tell old stories. We knew they weren't true. But it was fun to think they were. And whatever you believe is true for you." He smiled at the two children. "I'm going to pretend I believe it too. Of course, just as soon as I hear that someone is looking for a boy and girl in strange pantaloons, I'll have to say good-bye to you."

Vrouw Maarten was shocked. "Hendrick! You mean you aren't even going to *try* to find their parents?"

Heer Maarten didn't answer right away. He reached over to feel the zipper on Timothy's knitted shirt. Timothy showed him how it worked.

"Of course I'll ask around, Jannetje. Meantime it's nice to have children in the house again. Now, how about supper?" Heer Maarten stood up. He walked to the fireplace to knock the ashes out of his pipe.

Vrouw Maarten spread a white tablecloth on the long table. She showed Sarah where the pewter spoons were kept in a polished wooden box. When the table was set with blue and white plates it looked very pretty. Sarah ran outside and picked a bunch of daisies from a patch beside the front stoop. Vrouw Maarten put the flowers in a bowl in the middle of the table.

Timothy and Heer Maarten had gone to the barn. When supper was ready Vrouw Maarten sent Rachel to call them. Timothy came running out of a stall in the corner.

"Guess what, Sarah. I milked a cow! I really did. It's quite a trick."

Heer Maarten came out of the stall after Timothy. He was carrying two pails of foaming milk. "Your brother's very quick to learn," he said.

The milk was stored in a little wooden shed by the spring at the back of the house. Before Timothy came into the house Heer Maarten asked him to take off his sneakers. They were dirty from the barn. Heer Maarten slipped out of the wooden shoes he was wearing. He left them with Timothy's sneakers on the stoop.

Heer Maarten put on the soft leather shoes he had left just inside the door of the house. Vrouw Maarten handed Timothy a pair of scuffed slippers. "They belonged to my son when he was a boy," she said.

There was a pitcher of water and a basin on a stand in the back room. Beside it was a towel and a bar of brown soap. Heer Maarten poured some water into the basin. He handed

Timothy the soap. The two of them washed their hands.

Sarah had noticed another pair of wooden shoes on the stoop. "Do you always change your shoes when you come into the house?" she asked Vrouw Maarten.

"Yes. It helps keep the house clean," Vrouw Maarten said.

Sarah looked down at her sneakers. "I don't know whether these should be indoor shoes or outdoor shoes."

Vrouw Maarten smiled. "We'll decide tomorrow. Now sit down at the table."

There was salted beef, sausages, pickled pork, cabbage, beans, corn on the cob, and big loaves of crusty bread with sweet butter. Sarah was sure she had never eaten so much in her life. She could hardly cram down the raspberries and thick yellow cream.

After supper Heer Maarten and

Timothy went to put the horse into the barn for the night. Sarah helped Vrouw Maarten clear the table and wash the dishes.

When all the blue and white dishes were back on the sideboard, Vrouw Maarten walked over to the bed built into the cupboard in the corner of the room. "You can sleep here, Sarah."

Sarah peeked behind the curtain. The bed was a high shelf with a featherbed and goosedown pillows on it.

Vrouw Maarten pulled a low trundle bed from under the shelf. "This is what my son used to sleep on," she said. "I hope Timothy will be comfortable in it."

There were clothes of all sizes folded away in a big wooden chest in the back room.

"These were worn by my son," Vrouw Maarten told Sarah. "I'm saving them in case I should have grandchildren." She smiled. "My son was married last year. He has a farm in Flatbush."

"Flatbush!" Sarah said. "That's not far from where Tim and I live. I mean from where we will live." She stopped. "I'm not sure what I mean."

Vrouw Maarten changed the subject. "This is what I was looking for." She held up two linen nightshirts. "I'm sorry I don't have a nightgown that will fit you, dear. I never had a daughter. But you seem to be used to dressing like a boy."

Sarah and Vrouw Maarten went outside. Timothy ran out from behind the
barn. "Come and see the baby chicks,
Sarah."

After Sarah had looked at the chicks,
she and Timothy sat on the front stoop
of the house with Heer and Vrouw
Maarten. The birds twittered in the

summer twilight. It began to get dark. There were fireflies flashing in the peach trees around the house. Heer Maarten stood up. "Time for bed," he said.

Sarah thought Timothy would object to wearing a nightshirt. But he thought it was funny. "And it's cooler than pajamas," he said. He jumped into the trundle bed and was asleep almost as soon as his head hit the pillow.

For a long time after the candle was out Sarah lay awake in the cupboard bed. She wondered if her mother was worried about her. Then she remembered that in all the stories she had read about people going back into the past, time had stood still until they got back.

"If that's the way it is," Sarah said to herself, "it's not even time for supper at home." She closed her eyes and fell asleep.

Soon after breakfast next morning a farmer drove his horse and wagon down the dirt road to the gray clapboard house. Sarah and Timothy helped Heer Maarten and the farmer unload four sacks of corn from the wagon. The men carried the sacks to the millhouse.

Vrouw Maarten took Timothy and Sarah to see how the corn was ground. Neither of them had seen anything like the big round millstones. They stood and watched while Heer Maarten poured the kernels of corn through a hole in the upper stone.

"The grinding will take a while, children," Vrouw Maarten said. "Why don't you go and dig clams?" She gave them a round wicker basket and two long-handled spades. Then she walked back to the house.

Timothy and Sarah left the mill and walked across the beach. The surf slapped against the shore. High overhead in the blue sky sea gulls swooped and screamed. Now and then a gull dived down to grab a fish from the water.

Sarah and Timothy dug and dug in the white sand. They made a big hole in

the middle of the beach. But they didn't find any clams.

"Let's build a sand castle, Sarah." Timothy took off his sneakers and rolled up the legs of his jeans.

Sarah slipped out of her sneakers too. The warm sand felt good between her toes. She set to work to pile the sand into towers.

Timothy began to dig a moat. "I'm getting water," he said after a while. "Oh, rats. Now the sides are caving in."

Sarah looked up from the pointed turret she was trying to make. Suddenly a cold chill ran down her back.

Someone was leaning over Timothy — someone with straight black hair held in place by a strip of beaded leather. Except for a small leather apron and moccasins, he was naked.

It was an Indian. And he was holding a long knife!

Sarah felt as if she were frozen. She couldn't move or speak. Then the Indian stood up straight and looked at her. Now Sarah saw that he wasn't much taller than she was. He was only a boy.

"I never saw anyone dig for clams that way," the Indian boy said. "I don't think you'll get any."

Timothy looked up. He was so surprised that he dropped his spade. "Who are you?"

"I like to call myself Beaver," the young Indian said.

"I'm Tim. This is my sister, Sarah." Timothy stood up.

"Beaver," Sarah said, "will you show us how to dig clams?"

The Indian smiled. He picked up a spade and walked across to where the waves were lapping the edge of the beach. There he pointed to the wet sand. Sarah saw a little spurt of water. Beaver dug the spade into the place where the water had spurted. Up came a clam. It fell off the spade. Timothy made a dive for it. But the clam dug its way down into the sand before he could catch it.

Sarah ran to get the wicker basket. Beaver was already digging up another clam. As soon as the Indian pulled up his spade, Sarah shoved the basket under it. A fat clam fell into the basket.

Timothy began to dig with the other spade. Sarah was kept busy moving the basket from one to the other. If she wasn't quick the clam would escape. They lost more than half the clams they dug up. But there were so many in the sand at the water's edge that soon the basket was half full.

"It's my turn to dig, Tim," Sarah said. She handed Timothy the basket and reached for his spade.

The Indian laughed. "My people taught your people how to dig clams a long time ago. But you act as if you've never done it before."

Sarah spotted a little geyser. She dug her spade into the sand and came up with a clam. Timothy held the basket ready. Sarah tossed in the clam. Beaver stopped digging and watched her. When the basket was almost full, the Indian went to a pool left by the tide on the beach. He fished out a tangle of wet seaweed and crammed it into the basket with the clams.

"This will help keep the clams fresh," Beaver said. He put the lid on the basket and helped Sarah and Timothy drag it into the shade beside the millhouse.

"Whew! It's hot!" Timothy wiped the sweat from his forehead with the back

of his hand. "I wish we could go swimming."

Beaver stared at him. "Your people never go into the water," he said.

"That's what you think." Timothy pulled off his shirt and wiggled out of his jeans. He waded into the surf, wearing only his undershorts.

Sarah watched her brother splashing in the cool water. She wanted to join him. But she didn't like the idea of having to go around in wet underwear.

"Do you like to swim, Beaver?" she asked.

There was no answer.

Sarah turned to look for the Indian. She couldn't see him anywhere.

Just then she heard a shout. Heer Maarten came running across the beach toward them. He was very excited. "Tim," he called. "Come out of that water this minute!"

Heer Maarten was sure that going into the ocean was likely to give Tim a fever. Timothy and Sarah tried to explain that they often went swimming and it never did them any harm. But Heer Maarten wouldn't listen.

Timothy's wet undershorts were spread on a beach plum bush to dry. He put his jeans and shirt and sneakers back on.

Vrouw Maarten invited the farmer to stay for lunch. It was all ready in the house. They all went in and sat down. The miller's hair and eyelashes were dusty with flour.

"Did you find many clams?" he asked the children.

"Not at first," Sarah told him. "But then someone came along who showed us how to dig them."

"Oh, didn't you know how?" the farmer said. "I thought everybody did."

"The children come from over near Flatbush," Heer Maarten explained. "It's all forests over there, you know." He patted Sarah's hand to tell her to be quiet.

"Who showed you how to dig the clams?" the farmer asked. "There's not another house for miles."

"An Indian boy," Timothy said.

"Oh." Heer Maarten thought for a minute. "There aren't any Indians living around here nowadays," he said. "But some of them still come to get shells. Years ago they were always down at the shell banks making wampum."

"What's that?" Timothy asked.

"Dummy!" Sarah said. "That's Indian money."

"It's little purple and white beads made from shells," Heer Maarten said.

Vrouw Maarten interrupted. "We'd better hurry and finish eating. The tide is coming in."

Everybody stopped talking and rushed to finish lunch. Sarah wanted to help clean up after the meal.

"We'll do it later, Sarah," Vrouw Maarten said. "There isn't time now."

The farmer and Heer Maarten carried the bags of cornmeal from the mill to the wagon.

The sea was much higher on the beach now. It was crawling in a circle around the sand dunes.

Sarah went to take Timothy's undershorts off the beach plum bush.

The miller and his wife stood beside the dirt road and waved to the farmer as he drove away.

"Why did he have to leave in such a hurry?" Timothy asked.

Heer Maarten pointed down the road that led across the salt marsh. "Look."

Timothy and Sarah saw that the sea was washing across the road. Now that the tide was in, the house and the mill were completely surrounded by water.

They were on an island.

By the end of the week Sarah and
Timothy felt as if they had never lived
anywhere but in the gray clapboard
house on Mill Island. There were lots
of chores to be done. Timothy took the
cow to the pasture in the morning and
went to get her before supper. He
pulled weeds in the cabbage patch and
carried water from the spring to the
house. Sarah learned to make butter and
cheese. She sprinkled clean sand on the
wide planks of the floor and swept it
into patterns with a broom made of
twigs.

At breakfast on Sunday morning Heer
Maarten told the children, "There's no

service at our church here in New Amersfoord this week. I thought we might drive over to Flatbush to see Hans and his wife."

Vrouw Maarten looked very happy. "Hans is our son," she said. She looked at Sarah. "Those clothes need washing. Why don't you wear the dress I made for you?"

Sarah took off her shirt and jeans. She poured water into the basin on the washstand and scrubbed herself all over. Vrouw Maarten gave her white linen underclothes to wear. Then Sarah put on the long blue dress Vrouw Maarten had made from one of her own.

Vrouw Maarten brushed Sarah's hair and made two neat braids. "You look like a different girl," she said.

Timothy changed into a long-sleeved shirt and baggy knee breeches which had been carefully patched. The clothes felt strange. But they were fresh and clean.

Both Sarah and Tim wore wooden shoes. They had been wearing them for a week now and were getting used to them. Vrouw Maarten had scrubbed their sneakers clean. She said they made very good house shoes.

When the tide was out, Heer Maarten hitched up the horse and wagon. His wife climbed up on the seat beside him. Sarah and Timothy sat in the back.

They drove across the salt marsh and then past fields of long grass. A few miles down the road they came to a little wooden church.

"The minister will come from Flatbush to preach here next Sunday afternoon," Vrouw Maarten told the children.

For a long way the ground was flat and without trees. Now and then they passed a farm house. Stone walls bordered the fields, and a grassy path ran along each side of the road.

After a while the road began to wind through a wood. It was cooler here. Sarah was glad. She was not used to wearing so many clothes in the summertime.

The road was hardly more than a narrow lane here in the woods. Low tree branches brushed against the wagon. The gray horse had trouble pulling it.

"Tim and I can walk," Sarah said. "Then the horse could go faster."

The children climbed down from the wagon. They raced ahead down the lane.

"Sarah, look what we have here." Tim turned off the lane into a little sunny glade. The ground was covered with low thorny bushes. They were loaded with ripe blackberries.

Sarah was following her brother. She

picked a juicy berry and popped it into her mouth. "M-m-m. Let's pick some for a surprise for Vrouw Maarten."

"What will we carry them in?" Timothy asked.

Sarah stopped to think. If she held up the front of her dress, she could put them in that. But the berries might stain the dress.

"I've got an idea," Timothy said. "What about putting the berries in our wooden shoes?"

The two children stared at the berries and wondered what to do. Suddenly Sarah heard a low growl. She looked up.

On the other side of the glade was a large bear. He began to walk toward them through the thorny bushes.

Sarah grabbed Timothy's hand. She stepped backward toward the road.

The bear began to move faster.

Timothy pulled his hand away. "Run!" He bent down, took off a wooden shoe, and threw it at the bear's head. For a minute the bear was stunned. Timothy pitched his other shoe and then ran after Sarah in his stocking feet.

Sarah reached the dirt road. She too slipped out of her wooden shoes. It was easier to run without them. Sarah raced across the road into the woods on the other side. Timothy was right behind her. The bear stopped in the middle of the road to sniff Sarah's shoes.

Timothy and Sarah ran along a narrow deer trail. They didn't stop to think where they were going. All they wanted was to get away from the bear.

Sarah held up her long dress to keep from tripping over it. She wished she was wearing her blue jeans.

The trail led to a rocky stream. Sarah bent down to pull off her socks. She lifted her skirt higher and waded into the water. "This will throw the bear off the scent," she told her brother. "I read it in a book."

Timothy looked at her with admiration. He too took off his socks and stepped into the stream. "What'll I do with my socks, Sarah?"

Sarah held out her hand. "Give them to me."

Timothy handed Sarah his socks. She tied all four socks end to end and then looped them around her waist. The socks had been knitted by Vrouw Maarten. Sarah knew she had better take

care of them. But they were much too hot to wear on a day like this.

The cool water of the stream felt good to their bare feet. They sloshed along for a long time without speaking.

There were bright red flowers growing along the edge of the stream. Thick oak and hickory trees grew close together on each side of the water. It was dark in the woods, but a little sunlight came through the leaves and glittered on the stream.

The ground was hilly now. The stream wound between steep banks. Then it grew wider and deeper. Sarah stopped walking when the water reached above her knees. She climbed up the bank and sat down on a rock. "We must have lost the bear by now," she said.

Timothy scrambled up beside her. "I think we've lost ourselves too, Sarah."

"Caw, caw, caw." A large black crow flapped over their heads.

Timothy and Sarah sat very still on the rock above the stream. They watched a deer with two little spotted fawns come down to take a drink. A breeze rustled the leaves of the giant oak that leaned over the water.

At last Timothy spoke. "What are we going to do, Sarah?"

Sarah had been thinking. "There's not much use going back up the stream," she said. "We might run into the bear again. I think we ought to keep going until we come to a farm house."

Timothy slid down the bank to the water. He made a cup of his hands and drank from them. Sarah wondered if she ought to stop him. Her mother had told her never to drink from a stream. But there was no other water here. Sarah was thirsty too. She went down to get a drink. The water tasted better than any she had ever had.

They walked along the bank. When they came to a patch of blackberries, they sat down among the brambles and ate. There was no longer any question of how to carry the berries. Timothy rubbed his stomach. "Much better than a wooden shoe," he said.

Sarah was quiet. She was wondering

what Heer and Vrouw Maarten would think when they found her wooden shoes in the road. She wished she could let them know that she and Timothy were all right. But even if they found a farm house, there wouldn't be a telephone.

She got to her feet. "Had enough berries, Tim? We'd better move on."

The two children walked among the cardinal flowers which grew along the muddy banks. Sarah heard a humming noise. A tiny green bird with a red throat was dipping his long beak into one of the blossoms.

There was no breeze now. The air in the woods was heavy and warm. Both Timothy and Sarah were uncomfortable wearing so many clothes.

They could see a wide patch of blue sky between the trees just ahead of them. Then the stream flowed into a little lake. A flock of mallard ducks with shiny green heads swam on the still water. Timothy pointed at them. "Those birds have the right idea!"

Sarah thought so too. She untied the belt of socks from around her waist and pulled the long dress over her head. Then she slipped out of the bulky underwear. A fallen log lay beside the water. Sarah folded all her clothes and placed them on the log. She ran across the narrow beach and waded into the water.

Timothy had a great many buttons to undo. Sarah was already swimming on her back and spouting like a whale when he came splashing into the water after her.

The sun was lower in the sky when Timothy and Sarah finished their swim. They shook themselves like puppies to get the water off. In a few minutes they were dry enough to put their clothes back on.

When they were dressed, Sarah said, "We've come to the end of the stream. Now let's follow the sun. We'll be going west that way, not just round and round."

They set off through the woods. Ahead of them was the tallest hill they had come to all day. "Why don't we walk around it, Sarah?" Timothy asked.

Sarah wanted to climb the hill. When she was halfway up the steep slope it began to remind her of another hill — one she knew very well. She could hear

Timothy slipping and sliding behind her.

Up and up they went. When they got to the top there was a little clearing. Sarah walked across it and looked out over the forests below.

Timothy came puffing over. "Hey, Sarah, this is just like Lookout Mountain in Prospect Park."

Sarah nodded. "I think it is Lookout Mountain," she said. "Someday our house will be out there where all those woods are."

Timothy grabbed her arm. "There's a house there now," he said. "Look!"

Sarah looked where her brother was pointing. A thin line of smoke was rising out of the woods. It was a little to the right of the direction that they had been going. Sarah held up the skirt of her dress and started down the other side of the hill. She stubbed her toe on a rock. "Ow!"

"Sh-sh!" Timothy warned her. "Even if this is Prospect Park, the bears aren't in cages."

The two children walked as fast as they could after they came down from the high hill. The ground was rolling now. They came at last to a path that led through the woods. Here they could go much faster.

The path led to a small open field. Around it was a fence of wooden stakes. Tall green stalks of corn grew in the field.

"It's a farm, Sarah," Timothy said.

Sarah looked for the farmhouse. At first she didn't see it. She walked around one side of the fence. Then, in the shadow of the trees at the other side of the field, she saw a small house, shaped like an upside-down bowl. It was covered with bark and dry grass.

Sarah walked slowly toward the house.

Before she reached it a rope came down over her head. It was pulled tight around her chest. Sarah could hardly breathe. She managed to turn around. But she stumbled over something.

It was Timothy. He was lying face-down on the ground. His hands and feet were tied together.

Someone was trying to push Sarah down too. She squirmed away. Then she saw who it was. "Beaver!"

The young Indian was reaching out to grab Sarah. At the sound of his name he stopped and stared into her face. "Sarah!" he said. He stepped back. "What are you doing in those clothes? I didn't know you."

Beaver wiped the sweat from his forehead.

Now Sarah saw that his hand was shaking. His face was streaked with dirt.

"Something's wrong, Beaver," Sarah said. "Take these ropes off Tim and me and tell us what's the matter."

Timothy rolled over onto his back. He

watched as Beaver untied the rope from around Sarah's chest. Then Timothy raised his feet in the air so the Indian could untie them. Sarah bent over her brother and undid the ropes that bound his wrists together.

"I thought you were a friendly Indian," Timothy said. "Even if you didn't know it was Sarah and me, why would you do this?"

"If someone dragged away your family to make slaves of them, would you be friendly?" Beaver asked.

"Who would do a thing like that?" Sarah said.

Timothy got to his feet. "Who did it, Beaver?"

"The palefaces," Beaver said. "They came rowing in from a big ship in the bay. I was behind a big rock cleaning a fish I had caught.

"The rest of my family was digging

clams on the beach. My father went to greet the strangers. They pointed a gun at him. Then the palefaces put all my people in their boat and rowed away."

Sarah was sure that people like Heer Maarten would never do anything like this. But the Indian told her, "You can't trust palefaces."

"Why do you trust us?" Sarah asked.

"I don't know. You seem different from all the others," Beaver said. "What are you doing here? It's a long way from where I met you. And why are you in these clothes? I like your other ones better."

"So do we," Timothy told him.

"If you really want to know how we came here," Sarah said, "we might as well tell you."

The three children sat cross-legged

in a circle under a hickory tree. Sarah told Beaver how she and Timothy had stepped back in time to live in the gray clapboard house with the miller and his wife. Beaver listened and nodded his head. He did not seem to find the story hard to believe.

Then Timothy told about the bear and how they were lost in the woods.

While they were talking a black cloud had come over the sun. Far off there was a rumble of thunder. A few raindrops splashed down. The sky grew darker and darker. Then a flash of lightning lit up the wood. Crack! It sounded as if a tree had crashed to the ground. The rain began to come down harder.

"Come." Beaver ran toward the little house. The doorway was covered by a flap of bark. It was so low that Beaver had to stoop to go into the room inside. Timothy and Sarah came in after him.

Once the three children were inside the house, the door flapped shut behind them. Timothy straightened up and looked around. "This is neat, Beaver."

The Indian boy smiled. "I helped my father build it," he said.

A small fire burned in a pit in the center of the floor. Over it a hole had been left in the roof to serve as a chimney. By the flickering light Sarah and Timothy saw that the house had been made of a circle of young trees. They were tied together at the top with leather strings. The outside of the house was plastered with mud and covered with grass and bark.

There were benches around the walls.

Strings of fish and clams were drying on poles which stretched across the room. Beaver reached up and took down a large shad.

"I speared this one today," he said. "I was cleaning it when I saw the men come from the ship."

Sarah looked around for a frying pan. "How are you going to cook the fish?"

"Watch." Beaver pushed a pointed stick through the shad and laid it across the top of the fire pit.

"We cook wienies that way," Timothy said.

There was water in a large clay jug. Beaver dipped some into a clay pot and set it on the fire. He took a hard yellow squash out of a round basket.

"Let me help," Sarah said.

Beaver handed her his knife. She set to work to scrape and cut up the squash.

The thunder still rumbled through the forest. They could hear the rain beating on the outside of the Indian house. But inside it was dry. While the squash was cooking in one pot, Beaver boiled corn-meal in another.

There were no spoons or forks or plates. Beaver cut hunks off the fish and gave them to Timothy and Sarah. They ate everything with their fingers. Sarah tried dipping pieces of fish into the boiled cornmeal. She liked both the fish and the cornmeal better that way.

At least there weren't any dishes to wash.

While she was eating, Sarah was thinking. "Beaver," she said, "what were the men like who kidnapped your family?"

"They had swords and guns," the Indian boy told her. "Some of them wore gold rings in their ears and had bright colored cloths tied around their heads."

Timothy had seen men like this in the movies on television. "Pirates!" he said.

"Their ship is still anchored out in the channel," Beaver said. "I watched from the shore when they rowed away. Some of the men seem to be camped on an island."

"Could we swim to the island?" Sarah asked.

Beaver looked at her for a minute. Then he said, "I remember now. You're not afraid of the water like the other palefaces."

"They wouldn't expect anybody to

swim to the island then," Timothy said.

"It's too far for that." Beaver stood up and wiped his mouth with the back of his hand. "But I have a canoe." He went to the door to look out. "It's stopped raining."

He came back and pulled a large basket out from under a bench.

"What's in there?" Timothy asked.

"Clothes." Beaver took the lid off the basket. "In winter I wear more than this."

Sarah and Timothy came over to look at the soft leather skirts and jackets and leggings. Some of them were trimmed with shells and porcupine quills.

"Oh," Sarah said, "they're beautiful!"

Beaver smiled. He smoothed a little fringed skirt with his hand. Then he handed it to Sarah. "This is easier to move in than that paleface skirt you're wearing. Put it on."

Timothy took off the stiff shirt and baggy knee breeches Vrouw Maarten had given him. Sarah slipped out of the long, full-skirted dress. They changed into the soft leather clothes that the Indians wore. Everything was more comfortable. The moccasins were the best of all. Sarah liked them almost as much as her sneakers.

It was not yet dark outside. Timothy

and Sarah followed Beaver down the narrow trail through the woods.

Rain dripped from the trees and rolled off the leather jackets. The children dodged low branches and marched over a ridge. Beaver stopped at the top of a hill. He pointed in the direction of the setting sun.

Timothy and Sarah looked down at the water of the Upper Bay. A tall ship was anchored out in the middle. It was near a small, tree-covered island. Gray smoke curled up into the air from a fire burning there.

Overhead the clouds were pink. A wood thrush sang in the dusk. The bird had such a lovely trill that Sarah wanted to stand still and listen to it. But they had to get out of the woods before dark. She hurried after the others.

The hills dropped down to salt marshes near the shore. The children walked through long grass. They had to step on stones and fallen logs to keep out of the bog.

By the time they reached the water the sky was beginning to get dark. Beaver led them to a little inlet. A heap of driftwood and tangled grass was piled up near a sand dune. The Indian boy lifted a twisted piece of wood from the pile and brushed aside an armful of grass. "Help me."

Sarah pulled off two branches from the pile. Timothy scraped away a mixture of vines and weeds. Under everything was a canoe made from a hollowed-out log. There were paddles that looked like scoops inside the canoe.

Together the three children pushed the heavy dugout across the sand. They

slipped out of their moccasins and tossed them into the canoe. Then they shoved the canoe into the water and waded in after it.

When the canoe was in deep enough water to float without scraping the bottom, Timothy and Sarah climbed into it. Beaver gave the canoe a shove before he got in. He picked up a paddle and sent the canoe skimming out into the bay.

Timothy and Sarah paddled as hard as they could. They weren't used to the funny scoops. The canoe was very low in the water. But it glided along at a good speed.

The sky was almost black now. Stars began to show between the moving clouds. Beaver paddled toward a bright spark in the darkness. It was the pirates' campfire. Beaver used it as a beacon to guide them to the island.

For a long time the light from the campfire never seemed to come any closer. Sarah's arms were tired. She felt they had been paddling for ages. But she kept on lifting the paddle and pulling it through the dark water.

Then, far off, she heard music. Someone was strumming a guitar. The pirates were singing. As the children paddled, the sound came closer and closer.

The campfire was at one end of the island. After a while the children were close enough to see that the pirates were all gathered near the fire. Sarah couldn't see any Indians. Maybe the pirates had put them on their ship, Sarah thought. She looked over to where the tall-masted ship was outlined against the sky. A lantern swung near the stern.

Beaver turned the canoe. He paddled around to the end of the island farthest from the campfire. When the canoe was close to the shore, the Indian boy stepped into the shallow water. He signaled to Sarah and Timothy to get out of the canoe too.

The children dragged the dugout onto the beach. Beaver reached into it and took out the moccasins. They put them on and walked silently around the island on the soft sand of the narrow beach.

They crept closer and closer to the pirates. Soon they could hear them laughing and talking. But the trees were in the way. The children couldn't see into the camp.

"Wait here for me," Sarah whispered

to Beaver and Timothy. "I'll find out what's going on."

In the darkness she took off the leather skirt and jacket. She left them with the moccasins near a big rock on the beach and waded into the water.

Sarah swam around the island to where she could see the campfire. She kept under the water most of the time. Once in a while she stuck her head up for air and to take a look at the pirates. Beaver had told her palefaces never went into the water. The pirates would not expect anybody to be swimming in the bay. If they saw her, she hoped they'd think she was some sort of fish.

A long wooden boat was pulled up on the beach. About twenty rough-looking

men were near the fire. The man with the guitar was sitting with his back against a tree. A number of the men were drinking out of mugs. Some were singing. Two were doing a funny dance together.

At first Sarah thought there were no Indians there. But then she saw them lying on the ground near the trees. There were four of them, and they were very still.

Two of the pirates walked over to the

Indians. The shorter pirate pulled an Indian girl to her feet. The girl looked about twelve years old. Sarah saw that the girl's hands and feet were tied. She stood as well as she could in front of the pirate.

The music had died down. The guitar player was taking a drink. Sarah heard the pirates talking about the Indian girl.

"This one ought to turn out to be a housemaid, Tom."

"Maybe," Tom answered. "But Indians are not good servants. I don't think the captain will find a buyer for her, Jake."

"Why don't we just turn the whole lot of them free, then?" Jake asked.

"You'd better not let the captain hear you talk like that," Tom said. "He's a stubborn cuss. I'm glad he stayed aboard ship tonight."

The Indian girl stood in front of the two pirates. She didn't say anything. Jake looked at her again. "Sit down, lass," he said. "Sometimes I wish I'd never gone to sea." Jake walked over to a fallen log and sat down on it. He pulled a pipe out of his pocket and began to fill it with tobacco from a leather pouch at his waist.

Tom took his empty mug over to a keg of rum on the beach.

Sarah was beginning to feel cold in the water. She swam back the way she had come.

In the dark Sarah found her clothes where she had left them by the big rock. She put them on.

Timothy and Beaver had been waiting on the beach nearby. They came over.

"What's up, Sarah?" Timothy whispered.

"There are four Indians tied up on the ground in the pirates' camp," Sarah said.

Beaver nodded. "That's my family. Are they closer to the trees or to the water?"

"To the trees," Sarah told him.

"Is anyone guarding them?" Beaver asked.

"I don't think so," Sarah said. "The pirates are all singing and dancing and drinking."

Beaver thought for a minute. "Let's get our canoe ready to leave."

Sarah and Timothy helped Beaver push the dugout back into the water.

"Sarah, stay with the canoe and keep it from drifting away from the shore," Beaver said. "Remember, whatever happens, *don't leave the canoe!* Timothy, come with me."

Sarah climbed into the canoe and picked up one of the scoops. The two boys went back along the beach toward the pirate camp. Sarah dug one end of the scoop down into the sand to act as an anchor.

She waited alone in the dark. The pirates had stopped singing. The only sound Sarah heard was the slapping of the water against the side of the canoe.

Suddenly there was a yell. It sounded like Timothy's voice. Sarah stood up in the canoe. She wanted to go and help.

Then she remembered what Beaver had said. *"Don't leave the canoe!"* She sat down again and held onto the paddle. Her heart was banging inside her chest.

She saw the dark shadowy form of a man come out of the woods. He ran across the beach to where the canoe floated in the shallow water. Sarah held her breath.

In the distance she heard Tim's voice. He was yelling, "Help! Help!"

Sarah couldn't stand it any longer. She got to her feet and was going to jump out of the canoe. But the man was too quick for her. He waded into the water and grabbed the paddle out of her hands. Then he pushed her down in the canoe.

Sarah tried to get up. But another man had climbed into the canoe. He grabbed Sarah's arms to hold her down. She struggled. The canoe rocked.

"You stay still," a deep voice commanded. Sarah saw two more figures running across the beach from the woods. They splashed into the water and scrambled into the dugout. One of them picked up another paddle from the bottom of the canoe.

Now Sarah heard crashing noises in the woods close by. A rough voice called, "Which way did they go?"

Farther off, Timothy was still yelling, "Help! Help! Help!"

One more figure crossed the beach and climbed into the canoe.

This was what the others in the canoe were waiting for. They started to paddle away from the shore. Sarah opened her mouth to scream. A hand was clapped across it.

"It's all right, Sarah," a low voice said. "It's me. Beaver."

The canoe glided into deeper water. The rough voices were closer now. The pirates came crashing out of the woods onto the beach. But the Indians' canoe slid around the island and headed for the place where the pirates had built their campfire.

Sarah was sitting up. Even though it was too dark for her to see much of the other people in the canoe, she knew now that they were Beaver's family.

But where was her brother?

The Indians made no sound as they paddled along. Sarah knew she shouldn't talk. Beaver crouched in front of her in the canoe. He was staring at the shore of the island. They came to where they could see the pirates' campsite. Beaver whispered in the ear of the tall Indian who paddled the front of the dugout. The Indian signaled to the man at the back. The canoe turned and headed toward the shore.

Sarah looked at the camp. It was almost empty. The pirate with the guitar still leaned against the tree. But he had stopped playing. He was looking into the shadowy woods. Jake was sitting on the fallen log, holding a pistol.

The canoe came close enough to the shore for the two pirates to see it in the light from the campfire. Jake stood up and aimed his pistol at the canoe. The Indian behind Sarah pushed her down. All the others ducked. The bullet whistled high over their heads.

Jake was loading his pistol. Sarah heard a splashing. Someone yelled, "Here I am!"

Timothy was swimming toward the canoe.

The Indians paddled toward Timothy. Before they reached him Jake fired again. The bullet again went high over their heads. Either he was a terrible shot or he didn't really want to hit them, Sarah thought.

She reached over the side and pulled Timothy into the canoe. Beaver moved over to make space for him to sit down.

Tim was still wearing the leather clothes. The water was pouring off them. He was out of breath. "Boy, that was fun!" he said. "But I'd rather swim in a bathing suit."

All the Indians were paddling. The canoe raced over the water. The clouds had blown away, and the sky was dusted with stars. The Indian at the back of the canoe kept looking up at them.

"What were you screaming about?" Sarah asked Timothy.

"I was trying to give the pirates something to think about besides the Indians they had tied up," Timothy said. "While they were listening to me, Beaver slipped over and cut the ropes."

"You gave me something to think about too," Sarah told her brother. "I wanted to come and help you."

"That would really have messed things up," Timothy said.

"Why didn't you tell me what you were going to do?" Sarah asked.

"I didn't know. And Beaver told you not to leave the canoe," Tim reminded her. He yawned. "Let's not fight about it, Sarah. I'm tired." He leaned against the side of the boat and closed his eyes.

Sarah was tired too. She bent forward and rested her head on her knees. A moment later she was fast asleep.

"Wake up!" Someone was shaking Sarah.

She opened her eyes and looked into the face of the Indian girl.

Sarah sat up and rubbed her eyes. She felt stiff all over. Everyone else had left the canoe. It had been pulled up onto a beach. The Indian girl was standing beside the canoe and bending over Sarah.

"I am Beaver's sister, Running Doe," she said. "We let you sleep as long as we could. But the sky is gray in the east. Soon the sun will rise. We must go into the woods before anyone sees us."

Sarah stood up. She climbed out of the canoe onto the sand. While she stretched, the Indians pushed the canoe higher on the beach. They began to pick up grass and sticks to cover it. Sarah ran to help.

"This is my father, Brave Eagle," Beaver told her.

The tall Indian put down the piece of beach plum bush he had broken off. He shook Sarah's hand. "Thank you for what you have done for us. I'm sorry if I frightened you last night. I had no time to explain."

Beaver's father propped the piece of beach plum bush against the canoe. He pushed the broken end of the bush into the sand. A few branches were criss-crossed over the dugout and draped with vines. In a few minutes the canoe was completely hidden.

Timothy had taken off the wet jacket and leggings. Like Beaver, he now wore only a little leather apron and moc- casins. Beaver's mother, Moonglow, rolled up the wet leather clothing so she could carry it on her back.

"It will be stiff when it dries," the Indian woman told Sarah. "But I will stretch it with my hands until it is soft again."

Before they left the beach the Indian boy introduced Sarah to his grand-father, who was known as Star Watcher. He was a slender old man with snow-white hair and bright, dark eyes.

Brave Eagle started down a faint trail that led through the woods. After him followed Beaver, Timothy, Moonglow, Running Doe, and Sarah. Star Watcher was last.

Sarah would have liked to talk to Beaver's sister, who was right in front of her. But the Indians walked very fast and did not say a word. Every so often Timothy or Sarah stepped on a stick or crackled a dry leaf. The Indians never made a sound.

The birds were twittering in the trees. The sky overhead became brighter as the sun came up. They came to a ridge of hills. On the other side of it the trail joined another path. This led them back to the cornfield and the Indians' house.

The fire in the pit was out. Star Watcher had to rub two sticks together to kindle a new fire.

Running Doe sat on the ground outside the house. She picked up a stone rod which thickened into a ball at one end. With this she began to pound dried corn in a stone bowl to make cornmeal. Sarah wanted to help, but the Indian girl just laughed at her. "I can work faster alone," she said. "Tell me about yourself, Sarah. My brother said you come from another time. How can that be?"

Star Watcher had finished making the fire. He slipped quietly out of the house and stood beside Running Doe. Sarah had just started to tell how she and Timothy had stepped backward in time. The old Indian listened to the story. He watched Sarah's face all the while she was talking.

"I wish I knew how to get home again," Sarah finished. "I miss my mother and father." She was silent for a minute. "But I miss the Maartens too. I'm sure they're worried about us."

Just then Timothy and Beaver came running over to them. Timothy was holding a bow and arrow. "Beaver has been teaching me to shoot. Watch."

Beaver pushed a stick into the ground. Timothy fitted an arrow into his bowstring and aimed at it. Zing! The arrow flew past the stick to bury itself in a fence post.

"Let me try," Sarah said. Last year she had won first place in archery at summer camp.

Timothy ran to get the arrow. When he gave it to Sarah, she picked up the bow, pulled back the string, and took careful aim. The arrow winged through the air straight at the target. The stick split in half.

Beaver looked at his grandfather. "You see. She is not like the other pale-faces."

"Yes," Star Watcher said. "I do see." He turned and went back into the house.

Running Doe was still pounding the corn. "Star Watcher is very wise," she told Sarah. "He is the medicine man of our tribe. All his life he has studied the healing magic of plants. Did you see the little bag he wears around his neck? That is a charm. Long ago Star Watcher was given this charm by the old medicine man who served before him."

Timothy sat down on the ground beside Running Doe. "Is a medicine man the same as a witch doctor?"

"He can do magic," the Indian girl told him. "Last night Star Watcher steered our boat to safety. He drives away the evil spirits that make us sick. And he helps the corn to grow."

At this moment Moonglow pushed back the flap of bark that served as a door to the Indians' house. "Come and eat," she said. "I have cooked enough for everybody."

"Doesn't she always cook enough for everybody?" Timothy asked.

"My people eat only when they are

hungry," Beaver explained. "We each cook our own food. But you are guests. And my mother knows that we all must be hungry."

Moonglow had made cornbread. It tasted only half-baked to Sarah. But the Indians all seemed to enjoy it. Beaver ate three pieces.

All sorts of different things had been cooked together to make a sort of stew. Everyone sat around the pot and fished things out of it with a spoon. Then they ate with their fingers.

Sarah pulled out something that looked as if it might be a sparrow. She quickly put it back into the pot and took out something else.

Timothy held up a chunk of meat. "What's this?"

"Skunk," Beaver told him.

Sarah decided not to ask what she was eating.

After the meal Timothy went into the forest with Beaver and his father. They took their bows and arrows with them. Sarah spent the day helping Moonglow and Running Doe stretch deer hides until they were soft enough to make moccasins. Star Watcher went to gather herbs.

In the late afternoon Running Doe picked up a large clay jar. She started down a path that led to the woods.

"Where are you going?" Sarah called after her.

"To get water," the Indian girl said. "Do you want to come with me?"

Sarah followed her into the woods. The sun flickered through the leaves. A wood thrush was singing his little trill. A spring bubbled out of a hollow overhung by a large beech tree. Running Doe knelt down among the green ferns and filled her clay jar with water.

Then the two girls took off their moccasins and waded in the shallow stream that trickled from the spring. Cool mud oozed between their toes. A green frog darted out of their way.

Sarah wished they could stay in the woods. But Running Doe stepped out of the stream. "Come," she said. "Tomorrow you have a long journey. Star Watcher is going to take you back to your paleface friends."

Sarah put her moccasins on again. She and Running Doe took turns carrying the heavy jug of water. When they got back to the little house they found that Timothy, Brave Eagle, and Beaver had come home.

Timothy looked tired. "I've been

trying to walk in the woods without making any noise," he told Sarah. "I stepped on a dry stick when Beaver was aiming at a rabbit."

"Did the rabbit get away?" Sarah asked.

"Yes. I was sort of glad he did. But Beaver wasn't. He said *he* learned not to step on sticks before he was three years old. It made me feel dumb."

"Then maybe you won't mind that we're going back to New Amersfoord tomorrow," Sarah said.

"How?" Timothy wanted to know.

"Beaver's grandfather knows the way. He's going with us," Sarah told him.

"You mean the witch doctor?" Timothy whispered. "He's spooky."

Sarah put her finger to her lips. She too thought there was something strange about the old Indian. But she didn't want to scare Tim.

Timothy and Sarah slept that night in the little house with the Indians. Mats of woven grass were laid on the floor. Then they all lay down with their feet toward the fire.

Timothy fell asleep before Sarah did. She stayed awake listening to the strange sounds in the woods outside. An owl was hooting. The crickets were making a terrible racket. She heard what she thought must be a wolf howling.

Sarah rolled over onto her stomach and pretended she was in her own bed at home. The owl's hoots turned into the cuckooing of the clock in the down-stairs hall. The crickets became the steady traffic noises coming from Church Avenue. And the wolf's howling was the wail of a siren on a police car going down Ocean Parkway.

Sarah's eyes closed.

The next thing she knew, it was morning.

Star Watcher was already up. He was waiting for Timothy and Sarah. Moonglow had a bowl of boiled corn-meal ready for each of them.

The children changed into the clothes Vrouw Maarten had given them. Running Doe handed Sarah a comb and a mirror to use.

"I didn't know Indians had things like this," Sarah said.

"We trade furs to the palefaces for them," Running Doe told her. She helped Sarah braid her hair.

When Moonglow saw that Sarah and Timothy had no shoes, she let them keep the moccasins Beaver had lent them.

Sarah hugged the Indian woman. "I know how hard you worked to make them."

Moonglow smiled. "If you could stay with me, I would make you a beautiful dress," she said. "But Star Watcher says you must go."

The old Indian stood silently while the children said good-bye to Beaver and his family.

"Thank you for all you have done," Brave Eagle said.

Star Watcher started off at a trot down the trail. He didn't even look back to see if the children were following. They had to run to catch up with him.

In a few minutes both of them were

out of breath. Timothy slowed down. He began to trot, just as the Indian was doing. Sarah held up the long skirt of her dress and tried to keep up with the other two.

Hour after hour they trotted along. They left the trail and went into the deep woods. Star Watcher kept looking at the sun to make sure he was going in the right direction. Sarah was tired. Her clothes felt heavy and hot. Timothy wished he was still wearing only the little leather apron.

When they came to a small rocky

stream, Star Watcher turned around to look at the children. "Rest," he said.

Sarah and Timothy sat down on the rocks at the edge of the water. The Indian gave each of them a hunk of half-cooked cornbread and a piece of dried meat. "Eat!"

They chewed the tough meat and choked down the bread. Sarah saw that Star Watcher was bending over the stream to drink. "He must know if the water is safe," she whispered.

Timothy nodded. He cupped his hands and scooped up the cool water. "Great!"

Sarah had a drink too. The water washed down the food she had eaten. She felt better.

Star Watcher stood up. "We go on now," he said.

The children followed him through the wood. The ground was getting flatter. They came to an open meadow. The Indian started across it at his steady trot. Sarah and Timothy hurried after him.

The meadow was covered with rough grass. At one point they passed a tangle of raspberry bushes. Sarah wished that she could pick some of the berries. But Star Watcher was trotting even faster than before. Sarah held up her skirt and kept going.

The ground began to be marshy. The air smelled salty. Then, in the distance, Timothy and Sarah saw a big barn with holes under the eaves for the birds to fly in. There, by a dirt road near the sea, was a gray clapboard house.

Timothy and Sarah began to run. They raced past the cabbage patch and around the barn to the long front stoop of the house. Sarah banged on the door. Vrouw Maarten opened it.

For a minute she just looked at them. Then she stooped and hugged them both at the same time. Sarah threw her arms around her.

"Why are you crying?" Timothy asked.

Vrouw Maarten straightened up. She wiped her eyes with the corner of her apron. "We found a bear sitting beside your shoes in the middle of the road," she said. "We looked for you all day. I thought something terrible had happened to you."

Vrouw Maarten stepped off the stoop into the road. "Come, children. We must tell Heer Maarten that you are home safe." She walked to the barn. Timothy and Sarah came after her. "Hendrick!" Vrouw Maarten called.

Heer Maarten had just finished milking the cow. He came out of the barn. The old Indian followed him.

"Jannetje," Heer Maarten said, "look who's here!"

"Star Watcher!" Vrouw Maarten held out her hand. "It's good to see you."

"He brought back our children," Heer Maarten said. The miller put his arm around Timothy. He stroked Sarah's hair. "Let us all go into the house."

Sarah and Timothy left their dusty moccasins on the front stoop. Vrouw Maarten took their sneakers out of a chest where she had put them away. She looked at the clothes they were wearing. "Those need washing."

Sarah untied the sash of woolen socks from around her waist. Timothy was already unbuttoning his shirt. Vrouw Maarten had washed their blue jeans and polo shirts. She went to get them. Then she poured water into the basin on the washstand. She handed Sarah the soap. "See that Tim uses it too," Vrouw Maarten said.

Star Watcher sat at the long table in the kitchen-living room with Heer Maarten. The Indian spoke in a low voice. Heer Maarten was smoking his long-stemmed pipe. When the children came out of the back room, the miller turned to look at them.

Sarah helped Vrouw Maarten get supper. Star Watcher was the honored guest. During the meal Sarah and Timothy told of their adventures. Heer Maarten was angry when he heard about the pirates. "I'll complain to the governor," he said.

When the last crisp cookie had been eaten, the Indian stood up. He looked at Vrouw Maarten. "You are my friends," he said. "And I know you are fond of these children. My people and I are fond of them too. But they do not belong here."

Star Watcher walked to the fireplace. He took the leather bag from around his neck and opened it. From inside the bag he took a pinch of dried herbs. He threw the herbs into the fire.

At once the room was filled with thick black smoke. There was a strange musky smell. Sarah's eyes were stinging.

Timothy started to cough. He grabbed her hand and pulled her to the door.

The children stepped out into the clear air outside. They rubbed their eyes and looked around. Where was the road and the barn? Where was the sea?

Timothy blinked. "Sarah, we're back in the museum!"

Sarah walked slowly around the house. There were the cases of clothes and furniture. And there was the picture of the house as it used to be. She came back to the door and looked in.

The smoke was gone. No fire burned on the hearth. No dinner dishes remained on the table. And both the Maartens and Star Watcher had disappeared.

Sarah stepped inside the house. She started to walk into the room.

Smack! She banged into a glass wall.

Timothy came in and stood beside her. He tapped on the glass wall.

"We can't get back in," Sarah told him.

For a few minutes Timothy was quiet. Then he said, "I don't want to look at the mummy after all, Sarah. Let's go home."